MY UNSTOPPABLE MOMMY CAN COOK

Written By
Breeanna Hill

Illustrated by
Winda Mulyasari

Printed in the United States of America

First Printing, **2020**

ISBN: 978-1-7355328-0-6

Published by The Hill Mantle Company

www.breeannahill.com

Dedication

To Micah, Azaria, Ava & Elijah whose unconditional love catapults me into realizing my wildest dreams. To every Mother and Child who has ever longed to see themselves in a children's book.

This Book Belongs To:

_____

My unstoppable mommy can cook.

Mommy, what's that you're cooking?

Well, baby girl, we've got drumsticks, corn-on-the-cob & baked potatoes on the grill.

It looks delicious!

It'll be ready for dinner in no time!

My unstoppable mommy can cook.

Today I saw her watering leaves in the sink.

Mommy, what's that you're cooking?

Well, baby girl, I'm making collard greens.

Oh! Can I watch you?

Of course you can!

My unstoppable mommy can cook.

Tonight, we had so much fun making pizzas.

Mommy, what's that you're cooking?

Well, baby girl, I'm putting toppings on my pizza.

What's your favorite topping?

Some of.... thisss!

My unstoppable mommy can cook.

This morning, I could smell her famous homemade biscuits.

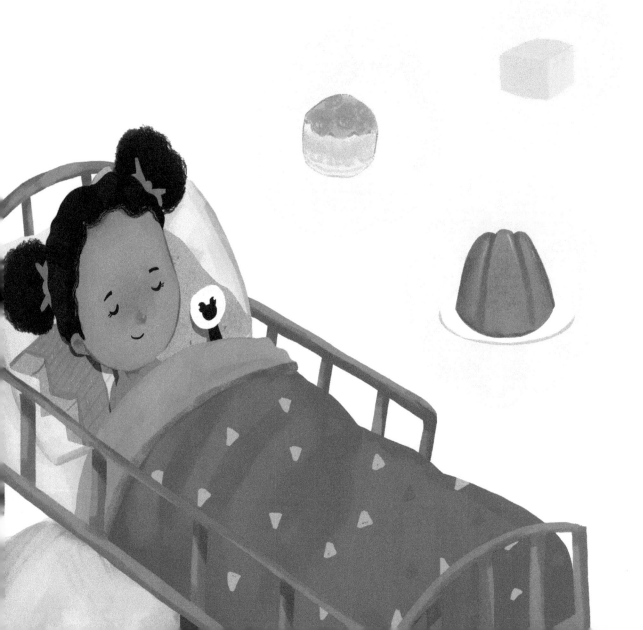

Mommy, what's that you're cooking?

Well, baby girl, why don't you take a wild guess?

My unstoppable mommy can cook.

On cold days, she makes yummy soup.

Mommy, what's that you're cooking?

Well, baby girl, it's the perfect day for yummy
soup & grilled cheese.

Mmm... I love extra cheese on mine!

Extra cheese coming right up!

My unstoppable mommy can cook.

This is my favorite time of year.

It always makes me feel good when we pull out our fancy dishes.

Mommy, what's that you're cooking?

Well, baby girl,
these are all of our
Thanksgiving favorites.

Did you see the pound cake
& hot water cornbread?

My unstoppable mommy can cook

Birdy & I are practicing
cooking like my Mommy.

Birdy, come look...

We have some popsicles, cake, hamburgers, bread & turkey.

My unstoppable mommy can cook.

I washed my hands really good so I can touch all of the vegetables.

Mommy, what's that you're cooking?

Well, baby girl, I'm making a salad to go with our dinner tonight.

Can I help you?

How about you hand me that tomato?

Ok, Mommy!

My unstoppable mommy can cook.

Daddy is going to help me make mommy a surprise dinner.

Ok Daddy, are you ready?

My unstoppable mommy can cook.
Mommy, Mommy close your eyes!

CPSIA information can be obtained
at www.ICGtesting.com
Printed in the USA
JSHW041023170920
7929JS00007B/5